# The Ways We Use Water

Matthew Bates

I0807045

Infomax Readers

Rosen Classroom™

New York

Published in 2013 by The Rosen Publishing Group, Inc.
29 East 21st Street, New York, NY 10010



Book Design: Michael Harmon

Photo Credits: Cover Chev Wilkinson/Stone/Getty Images; p. 4 Ikunl/Shutterstock.com; p. 5 (glass) Elena Elisseeva/Shutterstock.com; p. 5 (swimmers) Zurijeta/Shutterstock.com; p. 6 Peter Dazeley/Photographer's Choice/Getty Images; p. 7 Payless Images/Shutterstock.com; p. 8 flashgun/Shutterstock.com; p. 9 Gorvik/Shutterstock.com; p. 10 Yuri Arcurs/Shutterstock.com; p. 11 Maximus Art/Shutterstock.com; p. 12 © iStockphoto.com/poco_bw; p. 13 © iStockphoto.com/gchutka; p. 14 Johnny Habell/Shutterstock.com; p. 15 Paul Burns/Photodisc/Getty Images; p. 16 JaySi/Shutterstock.com; p. 17 Digital Vision/Digital Vision/Getty Images; p. 18 © iStockphoto.com/gradyreese; p. 19 © iStockphoto.com/nicolecioe; p. 21 MaxyM/Shutterstock.com; p. 22 (tubing) Bull's-Eye Arts/Shutterstock.com; p. 22 (jetski) YanLev/Shutterstock.com; p. 22 (canoe) Tyler Olson/Shutterstock.com; p. 22 (water skier) teekaygee/Shutterstock.com.

ISBN: 978-1-4488-9013-2
6-pack ISBN: 978-1-4488-9014-9

Manufactured in the United States of America

CPSIA Compliance Information: Batch #WS12RC: For further information contact Rosen Publishing, New York, New York at 1-800-237-9932.

Word Count: 302

# Contents

## Water Is Important

What's the most important thing on Earth?

Did you say water?

You're right!

We use water in many different ways.

We use it at home.

We also use water to have fun.

Water is important

because we can't live without it.

We drink water so our bodies work right.

Water comes to our homes through **pipes**.

We get water from a **faucet**.

Water tastes great!

We use soap and water
to clean our bodies.
Taking a bath uses water.
The soap and water make bubbles!

We use water when we wash our hands.

It's important to wash your hands

when they're dirty.

Washing helps us stay healthy.

We need water to clean our houses, too.

We use water to wash dishes.

We also use water to clean the floors.

## Watering the Plants

We use water

when we care for our plants.

Plants need water to live.

We water plants with a watering can.

The plants also get water when it rains.

## Working with Water

Sometimes, people work with water.

Can you think of someone who uses water at their job?

Firefighters put out fires with water.

This is a very important job.

**Gardeners** use water, too.

Gardeners take care of plants.

They need a lot of water to keep their plants healthy.

## Having Fun with Water

We use water to swim.

Swimming is fun.

It helps keep you healthy.

Sometimes, you swim in a pool.

You may have a pool at home.

Your school may have a pool.

Other times, you swim at the beach.

We go to the beach in the summer.

There's a lot of water at the beach!

We also play with water.

We use water to make water balloons.

It's fun to throw them outside!

# Different Ways to Use Water

drinking

using it at work

putting out fires

staying cool

gardening

watering the plants

having fun

swimming

going to the beach

Water is everywhere.

It's in our homes and towns.

It's all over the world.

Why is water important?

How do you use water?

# Glossary

**faucet** (FAW-suht) Something that gives us water when we turn it on.

**gardener** (GAHR-duh-nuhr) A person who takes care of plants.

**pipe** (PYP) Something that carries water to our house.

# Index